STORY OF A YOUNG

AMERICAN GAY PORN STAR

STORY OF A YOUNG AMERICAN GAY PORN STAR

Julian Black

AuthorHouse™ UK Ltd.
1663 Liberty Drive
Bloomington, IN 47403 USA
www.authorhouse.co.uk
Phone: 0800.197.4150

Published by AuthorHouse 09/09/2014

ISBN: 978-1-4969-8786-0 (sc)
ISBN: 978-1-4969-8788-4 (e)

The life of a young American gay porn star.

This story is totally fictitious and is made up from my own Imagination and is in no way shape or form about any person alive or dead if there is any similarity in the story to any person living or dead then it is totally coincidental.

I just wanna fucking dance

Alison Jiear.

My name is Cory and I am 20 years of age and my occupation at the moment is a gay porn star. I grew up in Oregon, Salem, my parents owned a farm and I was an only child. I kind of grew up always knowing I was different to the other kids in Salem because I never had any confidence or self esteem where the other kids would fight and mess around and kiss the local girls I kind of kept away from all of that and preferred to just watch in the background.

I was always effeminate and not camp I was just girly to the other boys you know and I think in a way the other guys in my area kind of picked up on this. I was called faggot a lot and faggot boy is coming you know and I guess I knew then that I was different to other boys my age.

I kind of kept to myself and had one or two close friends who would come up to the farm about twice a week and have supper with us but it got to a point where they did not really bother in later years because I was just deemed odd and faggoty and I guess they did not want to bother with somebody like this.

My parents are very religious and strict folks and I kind of grew up not being able to talk to them or communicate with them about things that I needed answers too in my life growing up. I remember my parents taking me to see my doctor when I was about 10 or 11 because I kept to myself a lot and would not socialise and stayed in my room a lot and the doctor referred me to see a psychiatrist (shrink). I was with him for about 6 weeks and he just told me to attend more social events and make more effort with the other kids. I told him but they just don't understand me, and he said "well make more of an effort and you will understand each other". He ended the therapy by telling my parents that he felt there needed to be more communication between us and that maybe they should make more of an effort with me.

I would always help my dad out on the farm after school and on weekends not that I wanted too but I felt I should, we would sometimes sit down for a break and my dad would say to me "you haven't got to stay here and work with me you can go out with your friends", and I would reply "na your ok I cannot call them friends you know", my dad would look at me and I know he wanted to ask me something because he could see something different in me to the other guys and the local's could see something different too but the question would never arise and we just got back to work as usual.

I wasn't really happy with my life growing up because I was in the closet and afraid to ' come out ' to my parents I guess I kind of become aware of my sexuality at the tender age of 9 or 10 I just knew I fancied the other boys in ways I should not. The friends who came up to the farm I would sometimes have sexual thoughts about them like when it was just me and a friend lying on my bed watching TV or doing our home work I would sometimes get aroused and when he was not looking I would stare at his butt for a few seconds and have thoughts of me taking off his pants and doing things to him which I cannot put into writing, I would always control my urges and would lie on my stomach to hide anything protruding from my pants but it was very difficult to control myself and as I got older about 12 0r 13 and especially in the hot summers my friends would come up to the farm and take off their tops and nearly always I would get those thoughts in my head but this time sperm would come from me and I could feel it coming from me and think oh no, don't but out a little would come and I would make an excuse to go to the bathroom where there was wet and a smell of cum on my pants, I would wash myself and change but the urge to keep my hands and body to myself was unbearable when I was lying next to a sweaty guy with his top off and butt bulging like a giant peach through his sweaty pants.

It was then I decided not to have any more friends over at the farm because I was afraid my sexual urges might take over me and I would then be in deep deep trouble.

I think the friends I did have kind of knew anyway that I might want more than friendship from them and when we stopped talking in school I think they kind of knew what it was all about, it was just a shame they were not like minded to me but that's the way it goes in small towns I guess.

So I became a loner and had no friends at all and after school just kept to the farm and became kind of Isolated, there was a local girl who used to come around to the farm now and again and I think she fancied me but as you can imagine it was not mutual.

I decided to do a very brave thing and I joined an LGBT group in our city I researched where I could find one of these groups and I met up with the LGBT leader and told him that nobody understands me and I cannot find anybody who has the same interests as me or thoughts like me. He then went deeper obviously and said what do you mean then by thoughts like you have? Well I said you know? No he said I need you to tell me. Well I said I have thoughts that no other guys I know do. "Oh really" he said. He said so you're telling me you have thoughts of guys of a sexual nature right? I shyly said well yes!

The advice he gave me was to be myself at all times and I could ' come out ' to my family and friends only when I am ready and he said you will know when you are ready then you will be able to go on and be intimate with guys and be happy with who you are ok.

He asked me if I had ever been intimate with a girl or guy and I told him no because I had never had any confidence or self esteem to go to that level and it was petrifying to me. He then went on to say that that is ok too because if you are not ready to be intimate with somebody and you just do it for the sake of doing it then I would probably not enjoy the sex and just be doing it because I would have been very very unhappy.

So he said it is a good thing you are sorting yourself out now because then once you are happy with yourself and you accept yourself and your sexuality then you can go on to like yourself and be intimate with people who you find attractive and who you have a connection with you understand.

He Said "Look Cory what I can do for you is to get you to join our weekly groups you can come along here once a week and talk to other people who have very similar problems to what you do, we just sit in a circle for an hour and just discuss ourselves and why some of us have some problems with our sexuality. We basically have a laugh and try to make sense of our fears and negativity towards our sexual orientation and by talking and taking advice from others who have been there it kind of turns into a positive or we try to turn it into a positive. But I always maintain that it is you who have to get acceptance for who you are in your own time and in your own way and you only we just try and make life easier for you by helping you out along the way to hopefully make the 'coming out' process more easier for the Individual."

Ok I said I will certainly think about it and let you know. There was no way I was going to join any group like that what if somebody knew me from Salem? What if I felt uncomfortable there and felt I did not belong in such a group? No I must do this in my own way and I think I know a way of coming out to the world and have lots and lots of sex in the process, there I will meet loads of guys who are not struggling with their sexuality or afraid of who they are but just shag the hell out of loads and loads of guys (why do I have such an urge to join the gay porn Industry an Industry I am so afraid of yet long to belong too). (Why do I want to go a lot further than most other people and be so dirty and have my body used as a sexual object for guys of all ages?) I think it's about the money but also about the sleaziness of the Industry and being different and giving it a go). Why the fuck not give it a go! I cannot understand it. I am afraid of people seeing me in an LGBT group in Salem, yet I want to be a gay porn star for the world to see.

I must get these urges out of my head and behave respectably and think of my dignity right I am going to behave and be a virgin forever. Yes I will stay a sad lonely closeted virgin forever and forget about the big bad world of the gay porn Industry well and sex.

Boy did this last long!

I really wanted sex and I think deep down I was a very sexually active young guy with a huge sexual imagination and I was very jealous of the guys in the gay magazines and on gay porn DVD's and the Internet that I had hidden away from my parents in my room. I so wanted to have sex with all those guys and be ‘ out ‘ and be a turn on for all other guys. It was not fair to me that these guys were having lots and lots of sex and I was still a young virgin afraid of sex. I could not understand where they got the courage from to just be themselves and ‘come out’ to the world.

I often thought well did they live in small repressed towns and how do their families feel about it? I would just be so resentful of them because they had the courage to say fuck you all and this is who I am they were not only ‘ out ‘ about their sexuality but they were getting paid and having fame for having sex on camera too and they couldn't give a fucking shit because at the end of the day they were getting paid lots of money for having lots of sex. But I still could not get over how very brave these guys were because people they knew could watch them having sex whenever they wanted too and those videos and Images would be there for life.

After the talk with the LGBT guy life just went on as normal really for me little Cory just going to school and roaming Salem bored with the people there and bored with myself I was just a frigid 18 year old guy who wanted more out of life than what I was getting I was lonely and I was frustrated and I was angry at myself and the world because of my rigid routine of a so called life!.

Then a family moved into the next farm about 7 miles away from ours they had come from Alabama and wanted to work a farm in Salem I had heard from my dad that they had a son who was my age and my dad said as soon as they get settled we will go around there and meet them. I could not wait because it was somebody different who may just be like minded to me.

My dad and mom and I got into our truck to meet the new family on the next farm and I was very excited the new boy in town might be a huge soccer male macho guy or basketball womaniser but he could also be effeminate and different and strange like me.

We arrived at the farm and the family were in the barn they saw us and walked towards us they took mom and dad into the house and said to me "Dominic is in the barn painting go in and see him", "you're his first friend around here he will love to meet you", I thought painting already he must be macho oh no wait till he sees effeminate me,.
I walked into the barn and there was sun shining through a crack in the wood of the barn right onto Dominic I could not believe my eyes and neither could he. He was a gorgeous guy with a lovely body and a butt that stuck out of his tight pants, his eyes Immediately caught my attention because they were sky blue and his hair was jet black and combed

to one side with just a few strands of his hair over his fore head where he had been sweating from the painting in the barn, we did not speak for a few seconds because we both knew we were the same effeminate and faggoty as the locals would call it, I could not believe my luck a hunky guy who I already had chemistry with in just a few seconds of a stare was my new neighbour and I could not wait already to get him alone in my room where I had a feeling some sexual awakening might happen for me and bring me out of the closet.

We talked for a while about the local town of Salem and I told him what the school was like and what the locals were like and I kind of told him without saying it about the homophobia and how opinionated people were, he kind of caught onto it because I just said "the locals are ok but if you are a bit different like effeminate if you know what I mean", and he certainly knew what I meant because he said "oh I know what you mean I had loads of opinionated people in Alabama throw their opinions at me because of the way we are". I kind of looked at him and said "the way we are", come on he said, were gay homos, boy wasn't it a relief that he was up front about his sexuality and didn't beat around the bush or bullshit each other like I did to make the point I wanted to make.

We just stared at each other and I said" so you're 'out' about your sexuality", "oh yeah well my mom caught me jerking off over a gay magazine, I had no Idea the lock on the bathroom door was busted and well I was busted, my mom cried and my dad went berserk he ripped up my magazine and called me a sinner and I just curled up into a ball in the bath tub covered in cum just crying and dying of fear and embarrassment."

We talked afterwards and they told me to forget the whole thing and pretend it never happened and never think that way again but I put it to them straight that I am gay and there is nothing I or they can do about that.

So have you had sex as well then Dominic?, "boy yes of course he was a college jock and a lot older than me and boy was he big very big, he was a top and I am a bottom it was the fuck of my life I mean it hurt at first and I was scared but once you've done it it's pretty much the same every time."

"Are you a virgin then Cory?" "Yes I am" he was being very honest and it was only right that I should be too, "I can fix that for you boy, he said".

I said "you want to fuck me" "hell yes, he said, you fucking need it by the looks of things I'll do things to you that are bad because I am a bad Alabama boy.

My dad came in to the barn at this moment and we both just looked at the painting that Dominic was doing on the barn and he said "ok Cory, let's go", I said to my dad "is it ok if Dominic comes over some time", oh yes he said, of course he can in fact he said us folks are going out next Saturday for Dominic's parents to meet the locals so he can spend the night",.

Dominic just smiled at me with his wicked eyes and wicked smile my father walked away and Dominic blew a kiss at me I went blood red and just went along with it and blew him one back.

I got home that night relieved that I met someone like Dominic somebody who understood me and who I was and he was good looking to boot, I fell asleep clutching my pillow and dreaming about Dominic and I was happy which I had not been in a very long time for obvious reasons.

Dominic started High School and we were in the same class I was a little nervous about Dominic coming to my school because he was openly gay and because I already knew him I knew he would cling to me because he never knew anybody else there. I was right he never left my side all day we kind of stood out because we were both quite effeminate and others do obviously notice this, Dominic had a few kids from school say to him that they didn't like his deep southern accent (why I don't know), I guess they just like giving the new boy a hard time but apart from that nobody gave him a hard time over his sexuality.

I guess I was the one with the problem with my sexuality and just blamed other people for me not ' coming out ' but being with Dominic just made everything ok and I fancied Dominic like mad as well.

All of the week in school me and Dominic were inseparable and at last I had a friend that I could really call a friend and Dominic would always talk about how hot some of the guys were in Salem especially the college Jock's Dominic was definitely into the rough jock's rather than the average guy,.

I was so jealous of Dominic he was 18 and had lived so much already having had loads of sex and ' out ' about his sexuality to anybody and everybody he was so proud of whom he was and lived for the moment. I felt so inferior to him because I was 18 like him and had done nothing compared to him I was so in awe of this walking hunk of a guy who had the world at his feet.

Saturday night came and as planned my parents and Dominic's parents went out to meet some of the locals in Salem and they dropped Dominic off at our farm to keep each other company.

I was so nervous because there was deep chemistry between me and Dominic and I knew something sexual was going to happen between us tonight I just knew it, I showered to smell fresh and I was kind of sweating with nerves because Dominic was so sexually experienced and I was still virginal and afraid.

Dominic came straight upstairs and shouted out to me I came out of my room and said "here I am", Dominic came into my room and jumped on my bed and just lay there, "make yourself comfortable I said", "Come and lie next to me said Dominic"

I quietly walked over to my bed and slowly lay next to Dominic. Dominic let his head rest on his arm while looking over me with his big blue eyes "oh you're so cute Cory he said" "you know what said Dominic you have a lovely bubble butt which I have been thinking about all the time," "Oh I said I think my bum is a bit fat and it sticks out a bit," "why are you so hard on yourself,", said Dominic I said "I don't think I am hard on myself I just have a fat butt".

Dominic got up from my bed and took off all of his clothes he had such a great body on him and was well endowed he had a lovely butt as well and he just stood there and asked me "so what are you thinking" my cock stuck up through my pants and Dominic said "I think he said it for us".

I was really nervous because it was my first time and everything and Dominic was so experienced sexually, I said "why don't we watch a DVD and have some pop corn" Dominic's cock was erect and his body was so firm I nervously lay down next to him we were both sweating from excitement and Dominic lay on top of me and took control and took my virginity.

We had nonstop sex for almost 2 hours (using condoms of course) and I could not get enough of Dominic he knew how to pleasure me and showed me how to pleasure him in every way he liked. We knew our parents would not be long so we both took a shower and I quickly hid my bed clothes under my bed and put fresh sheets on for obvious reasons.

We both got dressed and just talked for a while until our parents arrived at the farm Dominic asked "how do you feel", and I just said "different somehow like I am a man now and not a young inexperienced boy and my ass hole burns and hurts like a son of a bitch you ass hole "we both laughed!.

Dominic said "you know what is next don't you", I said "what", he said "you have to tell your folks that you're gay and 'come out' to them right."

'Come out' to my folks no way man," "Look said Dominic they know anyway it's just you have to be the one to confirm it to them".

The truck pulled up outside the farm and Dominic gave me a kiss and then said "hey I really enjoyed tonight" I said yeah I did too and thanks for well taking my virginity my farts hurt like hell but thanks anyway" "your farts smell like hell said Dominic and down he went to greet his parents".

I got undressed and got into bed my mom came in and said "good night" and that Dominic is good for me", whatever she meant by that. I felt like a new guy who was now no longer a reserved virgin but" sexually experienced "by a guy who taught me what sex is all about, I loved Dominic and he will always be the guy who broke me in so to speak and gave me an ass hole, but I wanted more than the local guys from Salem, Oregon and the new guy from Alabama and working on a farm like my dad. I wanted to leave my small town and go to Los Angeles where all the fun was and all the hot guys were and that is where I wanted to live and work in the back of my head was the sex Industry because I wanted to do something that was way out there and different but I was a young guy wanting to enter a world that would totally take me by surprise in every way imaginable but a world I would adapt too just because I learned too.

I decided to tell my mom and dad the following day I was gay Dominic's courage's attitude to life gave me courage and I just sat them both down and took Dominic's advice and just came out with it because I didn't want to leave it any longer to tell them my news. They both just stared at me and said to each other" well our suspicions were right our son is gay "I replied ye and well there it is". My mom said "well it explains the isolation and difference in you as of late anyway".

"Look they said are you happy with being gay "I replied ye I mean I wasn't but that changed", "through Dominic right said mom" I replied "you know that Dominic is gay" "oh come on Cory said my mom of course we knew like we suspected you for some time now".

"But you never said anything" "because we were waiting for you Cory to say it" oh I said. My dad asked me to keep it quiet where other members of the family are concerned and I said that is fine.

I called Dominic straight after and told him my news and said "is that shag still available" "of course get your ass over here and we'll celebrate with your ass. "In Alabama style of course."

Myself and Dominic had wild erotic sex and I now felt free and more accepted of myself because I was now myself and I guess ok with that. After our many hours of sex (Dominic's parents had gone out by the way), I told Dominic about me wanting more out of life and to not just work on a farm day in and day out like my dad.

I said I wanted to go to Los Angeles and be a gay porn star I always wanted a lot more out of life and I wanted to work in an Industry that was very much bigger than life and way way out there. Dominic said "wow Cory do you kind of know what you are doing here, I mean I know nothing about the porn Industry but well hey the porn Industry".

Dominic said "look let me get some of my contacts in Los Angeles and I will look into it for you I mean, hey look you're a young inexperienced guy from Oregon going into Los Angeles and the gay porn Industry". I said "you have contacts" well said Dominic "I may know somebody who knows somebody let me get back to you.".

Cory from Salem, Oregon going to be a gay porn star well who would have thought.

Three days went by and Dominic got back to me we met in the local cafe and he told me that he had a friend in LA who knew somebody who had been in the gay porn Industry for about two years now and Dominic had a contact number for me and some advice. he said "Look first off you have to call them and tell them a little bit about yourself then the next step is you go to their office and they put you through the "casting couch", where you strip and there is a guy there who will take some snaps of you and then perform sex on you to see if you fit into the category of 'gay porn star'."

"You're young well hung (well of average) and you're cute but to me you lack confidence and self - esteem and I feel you don't know what profession you're going into, I just feel it is so not for you."

I said "Dominic why are you putting the flames out on this one for me I really want to do this as a career and become a huge gay porn star. I mean others do it my age and they get famous and guys love them forever".

Dominic said "look I am not putting you down Cory but do you really want to be known as Cory from Salem who has sex with loads and loads of guys for cash you'll have your naked body all over the Internet and on DVD's for the whole world to see and we will just tap in your name and see you fucking guys all over the place is that what you want". "I mean what about your family and the locals and your school friends what will they have to say about Cory the gay porn star."

"I just don't feel this is you Cory at all".

"So what about your friends dude in LA he must enjoy It. "hey man he is way out there and confident and wild and can handle the sex Industry from what I am told"." So does he just do porn for a living". "No he has just got his degree from university and is going to be a veterinarian. I am told it was just to get him through college but apparently he is going to be doing more porn too man."

"I guess you will get to met him if you get into the Industry and end up fucking him look man I really think you need to think this through I mean the gay porn Industry Cory the gay porn star ha ha man.".

"Look Dominic I really want to do this and it is all I want to do I will get to fuck loads of good looking guys with huge cocks and get paid for it in the process it's what I want it's who I want to be and I am going for it what the fuck is wrong with Cory the gay porn star, what the fuck is so wrong with that."

"I watch gay porn man and I love to watch it because I am a gay guy who loves watching guys fuck each other and moan and groan in the process and I wank off to it that's what it's there for right, but Cory I sometimes look beyond it and I see young guys like yourself and I look at their faces at the end of being fucked and fucked ragged they look sad and I almost feel sorry for them because they just look like vulnerable young gay guys who are just there to be fucked by other guys in the industry who ever that may be. (you may not even have a choice who you will want to fuck you it may just be there for you and you take it) can you really cope with that, can you cope with being fucked and then smiling at the end of it like you enjoyed it having a red sore ass hole and covered in spunk. "I just don't feel you can cope with it all Cory I really don't.".

"Listen these guys get paid for it and they get fame from it and they get to fuck fuck fuck", "Cory you have got to listen to me I know you and I can already see the sadness in your face and eyes after a sex scene it's not you man you're not Cory the porn star it's a crazy industry for people who just don't give a shit"

"I am going to Los Angeles and I am going to be Cory the gay porn star and nothing and nobody will get in my way, I'd love it if you will come with me you could be Dominic the gay porn star from Alabama, man my parents would flip out and my grandparents would say "Dominic I just don't know" I know my limitations and being all over the web having sex is not one of them". "This is not for you man believe me, the gay porn industry is just not for little old you! I just don't want to see you get used and abused and I don't want to see that vulnerable and sad look on your face that I see on so many other young guys in the Industry of gay porn after their sexual conquests or sexual commands and I don't want to see some huge big cocked hairy guy stroking your hair and arm like you're a little puppy ready to be well and truly fucked and I will look at you pretending to be happy about being a little skinny bitch for some huge hulk of a guy."

"It will not be like that I just know it will not be like that because it is my choice to have that huge big cocked hairy hulk to fuck me and I will be there by choice because it is the Industry I want to go into, and that Industry is to be fucked for money and fame and remember we are all consenting adults in this are you forgetting that".

"I think your forgetting your own fucking mind", "well Dominic it is my mind to forget and mine alone and I will make up my own mind so just back the fuck off ok".

"You might want to be known as Dominic the farm hand from Alabama who has moved to fun filled fucking Oregon, but I want fame and fortune in the tinsel town of LA. I want to be Cory the gay porn star who guys love to wank over and dream about!

I want fun I want to be fucked by loads of guys, I want the night life of Los Angles I want the apartment I want guys to see me and die and ask for my autograph, I want to live and I want to own the gay porn Industry and make it mine yes I will make it mine "and fuck anybody who doesn't like it".

"Do you know what you're fucking saying, ""I know what I am saying, I fucking know what I am saying "!

And it's my ass and I will do what I want with it!

I decided to tell my parents about my future plans to go into the gay porn Industry as you can imagine I was very nervous about this because how do you tell the guys who brought you up that you want to belong to such a vocation as this I just don't know?. I sat them both down or we were all sat down for dinner and I thought just come out with it Cory like you did when I ' came out ' to them, they had to deal with my sexuality and now they had to deal with this too poor things.

I just said "well guys I have decided what future I want to go into and it does mean moving from here to Los Angeles!"

My mother stopped eating and looked up at me "Los Angeles she said but that is a huge city a place your not used too Cory, what could be there for you". I just came out with it "well I I I um want to have a go at the um um well it is called the um or what is it called now or damn that is it the gay porn Industry yes the gay porn Industry," I did not look at them and pretended to do up my shoe lace I could feel myself sweating with fear. There was silence from my mother and father and I could feel them looking at each other in pure amazement.

"My father said" Cory do you know what you just said to your parents "I got up from under the table and my complexion was red and hot," yes dad I said "I want to try the gay porn Industry, I just have to try it ok and see if it is for me". My mother said to my dad "you have to stand your ground with this and say no to him we cannot possibly allow our son into such a sleazy world as that" "But it's not a sleazy world mom it's a future in it for some and it's making lots of money too in the process and it's a huge huge business.".

"Cory you're talking about shaming us with your body being used for sex for money how do you think people will react in Salem and how will me and your dad be able to show our faces in town again have you thought about us" "my dad said "you cannot do this to us boy what will the other dads say and the guys your friends it's that Dominic isn't it he's got these crazy ideas into your head your both going aren't you Dominic fucking Dominic I'm having words with his dad".

"Guys guys please this is not about you or about Dominic me and Dominic are not talking ok because he tried to talk me out of it this is not about you guys either it's about me and me wanting to have a go at this. I just want more out of life and I want to try this I know I am timid I know I haven't much confidence and I know what I am walking into here ok and I know what I will be walking away from too if it doesn't work out I just have to do this."

"My mom spoke up again but Cory you are not right for this this is not you you'll have your body all over the Internet and in magazines and oh my lord it's a sin it's a pure sin. Oh my lord what have we raised you were such a sweet little boy".

"Yes well I said most of the guys in the gay porn Industry were sweet little boys once life changes all that!"
"Look guys I am going to LA and I am going to try this and I so need your support on this because I am going whether you like it or not".
my dad said "ok Cory go but this is certainly not for you but if it's what you want then me and mom will not stand in your way or turn against you I mean if anything you will need our support to enter such an Industry. Don't worry about what people say if they should "find out" we will deal with it?"

“Thanks guys I have to do this”.

“Oh Cory said my dad where did you come from”

I said “I bet all the parents and family and friends of gay porn stars say that to them at some point or something a bit stronger”.

There was now no going back I was all ready to enter the world of gay porn and was I ready for this or was I not I did not have a clue myself but I had to try it like many many guys have both past and present. It has always been there and is a huge industry.

I got the e mail address of a gay porn studio and contacted them and was trembling doing it a few hours later they e mailed me back and asked my age and some other details. I put I was very nervous because I was and they e mailed back who isn’t Cory relax come down have a chat with us and we will see how it goes.

My folks gave me some cash to see me on my way and they said to come home if I am not happy at all or in any way the next thing a car pulled up at the farm and it was Dominic my parents had contacted him because they knew how upset I was that we were not talking. he said “oh man so you’re doing it your actually doing it” I said “ye here it goes” “look said Dominic give me a few weeks and I’ll come down to LA to see you I have some friends down there and

I have asked them to keep an eye on you maybe I am asking the wrong people here but take care okay, and give me just a few weeks I guess I'll see you on the internet well it isn't anything I haven't seen before right, we both laughed. "I said you can always say I had him first"

Dominic left and I shouted to him I'll text you, he shouted back you'd better!

My dad took me to the airport where I was now on my way to Los Angeles to be part of an Industry I was petrified of but loved at the same time I guess all gay porn stars feel like this because you just never know how you're going to feel about being a part of an Industry that few people ever talk about but an Industry that a lot of people go into because they want to try something that they are very curious about and try something different that they get cash for to pay the bills and get themselves all over the Internet in the process. But I feel you have to be a little mad and be of an eccentric nature and have a wild Imagination to be part of this and of course be sexually active too where anything goes but be intelligent too at the same time I was sure I fitted all of these things but was still scared of what lay ahead of me in the gay porn Industry.

I got to LA and rented accommodation and then made my may to the gay porn studio I was nervous but I was here and I needed to go through with this. I went to reception and gave my name and the young guy said to sit down and

I will be called. I sat down and the next thing a young good looking guy came out of one of the rooms he was doing up his belt and tucking his top into his jeans as he was walking out he looked warn out and tired and I thought he must have had an audition or something and as you can Imagine I was now very nervous and was I ready for this?.

My name was called by the receptionist and I must have looked very nervous and tense because the receptionist guy said

"Are you ok honey do you need some water" oh no I said I'll be fine, he must have seen people like me a thousand times over. I made my way into the room and there was a tall guy in the room wiping down the white sofa that was in the room and opposite was a glass desk with a pen and note pad on it. I now knew what had gone on just a while ago it was obvious to see this was no ordinary interview.

"Oh hi." he said, "You must be Cory my 11.30." "Oh yes" I said. Cory sorry he said I am just cleaning up from the last guy.

Oh I said right, ok he said sit down here and tell me a little about yourself. "Well" I said "I'm Cory from Oregon and well here I am." He said "why do you want to enter this Industry Cory "well I said" I have just always had a passion for it I guess just want to try it see what's it about".

Ok he said your cute which is what guys go for a nice rounded ass and slim body. Ok Cory he said "take off your clothes for me and give me a twirl". I kind of hesitated. "What's the matter Cory he said" I said well um all my clothes "well yes he said all your clothes. Right look Cory he said "I have not got time to sit here and talk to you and be your shrink you come into my office because you want to be a gay porn star for thousands of people to watch you and to make me and you money simple as you come here through choice through your own submission if I choose you for one of my porn stars you go on to have sex with lots and lots of guys. He was straight to the point and very firm with his voice.

Right one more time he said "Cory do you want to take your clothes off for me and show me your body if not please go now because I have a full day of appointments to get through I am a busy guy I do not have time for this you want to come into the fucking gay porn Industry for fuck sake taking your clothes off for me is just the start of what's to come.

I took a deep breath and started taking off my clothes after all If I walked out now that would be it and I was here standing in front of my employer. I took off all of my clothes and tried to relax. That's my boy he said!
He got up from his desk and walked over to me and started touching my body my shoulders, my stomach, my bum and I felt myself becoming aroused, oh he said "you like me

already" he was a big guy and well built and had a beard I was scared of him but yet aroused at the same time.

Relax Cory he said I can make you a star he told me to get on the sofa and go on all fours and spread my ass up in the air.

He stroked the cheeks of my ass and I felt his fingers touch the rim of my ass and I was hard and fully aroused. Ok Cory he said, I am not going to say what the audition was like but put it this way I had only ever had sex with one other guy now it was two he said "I am going to put you together with Billy and do a couple of scenes for me with him ok."

"Come in tomorrow at 9.30am we will go into the studio and we will do some scenes with the lovely Billy you will love him and we'll see what you have got." As I was leaving he said "Cory come in tomorrow positive and relaxed with a smile you are here because you chose to be here, if you want to stack shelves in the shopping mall or clean bathrooms then you know where they are you chose the gay porn Industry I need you to be confident and relaxed and looking like your enjoying it even if you're not. If you cannot give me this then I suggest you not turn up tomorrow ok Cory".

I looked at him and said ok see you tomorrow." hey he said "you'll be fine kid look how far you've got so far and he winked at me and said get out of here."

I got back to my hotel and lay on my bed and thought about what I had just done I had gone to a gay porn studio I had met and auditioned for a gay porn director who saw straight through me. I had stripped naked and I was sexually aroused by it and we had sex if he had brought in 3 guys to have sex with me I think I would have let them do it with just a bit of confidence I think I would be up for anything and a total exhibitionist I just needed a push my body was ready but was my mind and what would my mind and body feel like after doing all my scenes and being with all those guys and using my body in this way. What would be the after effects and why was I being so negative.

I got up the following day and just stared into an empty wall wondering what today was going to bring I washed changed and made my way to the porn studios where Billy was ready and waiting for me and so was our director. I was introduced to Billy and I could see straight away that he was confident with his body and his mind he was loud and a true exhibitionist he wiggled his bum at me and told me I was very sweet and handsome.

He was the total opposite to me and he was comfortable working in the Industry he was laughing and ready to get on with it.

"Ok said our director Cory Billy is going to lead the way and because this is your first shoot I have picked Billy to show you how it is done and Billy will just let you know

what positions where to kiss him he will guide you and give you your mark and I will just be with the camera and direct Billy who will then guide you, do you understand Cory any questions?"
yes I said "I am not doing any sex without condoms I just will not it is an absolute must for me it was what I was taught growing up in school" the director said "look at you already calling the shots of course we use condoms".

"Ok then said the director let's do these scenes and finish them it will be a 40 minute shoot Cory I want you looking happy and comfortable and like your enjoying yourself ok simple as I don't want you looking like I have just asked you to clean my toilet which is full of shit and blocked up ok you get me."

Billy laughed at what the director said and told me that I will enjoy it and he will make it fun for us both. Billy was only the third guy I had ever had sex with and this time we were being filmed and watched and Billy was a guy I had only known for about 20 mins.

We got on with the scenes and Billy whispered in my ear where I should kiss him and what positions to be in and the director would shout now and again Billy turn over Cory over Billy. Billy lying down Cory on all fours, it was tough work and some positions were painful to be in for too long but because it was pleasurable your mind was focused on the sex and the enjoyment of it. I learned to control my body by the power of my mind and would listen to commands from Billy and the director and would just follow instructions.

Every now and again I would feel like saying stop or running away but I learned to discipline myself to breathe and learn to enjoy it and just take the pain and go with the flow it was only for 40 mins and during this time you just learn to perform and enjoy.

The 40 mins were up and Billy and me were fucked out and we just lay on each other covered in spunk and our heart beats were just coming down from thuds which could be heard miles away. We were soaking wet and shagged by all standards.

Our director said "that's my boys and said ok guys this will be on the web and DVD so look out for yourselves it just hit home the web I am going to be on the web seen having sex by millions of guys I did not know how I felt about it but it was done and that was that. After all the sex it is then it kind of hits you after all the rush I always felt a bit guilty and dirty for doing these filthy scenes on camera for others to watch and often thought about my dignity and self respect or was I letting others opinions take over the way I want to live my life I was brought up in a very conservative family and environment and I think that was why I felt so guilty.

Billy gave me his contact details to go out for a drink some time there was a bit of chemistry between us Billy told me lots of guys meet through the industry and go on to have long lasting relationships and the sex with others is just a paid job.

I went home and had a shower and thought about my day and about my scenes and about the industry and It was not so bad really you just get paid for having sex and listen and enjoy the commands from a very controlled environment but I was not so confident as Billy and that did scare me Billy seemed like he did not have a care in the world he came in had a laugh and took off his clothes and went to work it was his job A gay porn star! and that was that he didn't make a bigger thing of it than what it was his theory was which he would say to me Cory in 100 years we will be dead rotting bone or powder dust if you want something in life go for it and do it we are not here for long. We all have one thing in common as human beings were all going to die one day so fuck the snobs and bigots of this world you're a gay porn star be proud of it!

That night the director phoned me to ask me would I do a few scenes tomorrow with me and five other men a gang bang with a story involved it would mean lots more money and lots more viewing and would make me a big star in the porn world I did not know what to say and was I ready for this kind of sex I went quiet and the director said to me" come on Cory don't let yourself down this could make you big in the Industry.

I said yes and thought oh boy what have I just done? My ass was already hurting from today and I was still fucked out what would five guys do to me and would I be able to take it.

I called the director and asked the ages of the five guys he said "let me look at my forms here 21 24 38 42 47 ok" oh I said he said "any problems Cory" no I said see you tomorrow oh he said "don't wank save your energy". As If I had the energy to cum after today. (Oh god what will tomorrow bring).

I got up the next morning and thought Oh god what have I said I would do today I got my shit together and headed off to the studio where again the director and five men were sat talking on the sofa "oh here he is said the director man of the moment" only to me it was ass of the moment just a piece of ass of the moment. I got Introduced to the five guys who were well built men and well hung too the director just took me aside and said "again Cory enjoy and go with the flow just let yourself go and enjoy cock just let your body go limp and enjoy".

We all took our clothes off and this time there were more cameras and more camera men which made me nervous I wasn't sure what I was doing but I just as the director said went along with the scenes basically once one guy had inserted his cock up me the hurt passed and the other 4 were not so bad after that we obviously used protection I would not consent to sex without it. We had dialogue at first like a mini story to open up the sex scene basically I was a closet gay who worked in an office and I was sexually frustrated and I was working with five hot guys who ganged up on me for being in the closet they then ripped my clothes off and I was fighting them but at the same time I was finding all this sexually stimulating and exciting they could see I liked them being forceful with me and I was hard and of course I just bent over the desk and let them take their turn with me that was the story in the end my character just lay in a ball because I was ashamed of myself for letting these guys have their wicked way and they all just wanked and cum all over me I end by saying "but I am not gay" which made all of us laugh.

I got up and was very sore and stinking of hot sticky cum but the work had been done we all shook hands and went our separate ways the director and camera guys now needed the studio for another shoot and two of the other gay porn guys were going to another porn studio to do more scenes and I thought fuck that.

I went home and thought well I am doing it I am a gay porn star and I am having lots and lots and lots of sex and getting paid for it I am actually out there living in Los Angeles and doing it working in the gay porn Industry. I had a text from the director saying your first scenes are now available to see on the Internet it has just got on there, I had a cold shiver down me and was scared to look I was now having sex on the Internet for the world to see and for people who know me to see and I thought well now will come the judgment from people I know and now people I know will know I work in the gay porn Industry. I typed in my porn stage name and sure as hell there I was having sex on camera it was that simple. (God help the next footage of me with five guys I just hoped and prayed my parents would never get to see me like this and I hoped they would not want to look anyway).

For me that was when it hit home that I was a gay porn star working in the adult entertainment industry up until the footage of me on the Internet I was just having sex doing my Job and nobody knew only me and the studio but now everybody knew who wanted to know.

I just didn't know how I felt about it having my body all over the web on adult gay porn sites I was lying on my bed and thinking about it but the thinking and the silence just made me worry so I called Billy and he said "what are you worrying about man your famous you moron he said I'm coming over man".

Billy came to my pad and I asked him how he felt about the Industry and about people seeing him (Billy was a total extrovert and exhibitionist and was full of confidence we were so very different but Billy told me "look Cory I come across as a raving mad queen who doesn't give a shit but I am sensitive deep down believe it or not and when I go back home to see my folks in New York I get some dirty looks and ignored by some of my parents friends and the friends I had in New York just stay away from me my parents don't talk to a lot of their friends now because of what they have said about me, and yes it hurts because they were my parents friends but my parents know it is my job and they know how much I enjoy it which I do I love having sex and I love getting paid for it even more it's my living and it keeps me here in Los Angeles with a roof over my head and food on the table it's my job simple as a job I chose because it was what I wanted to do."

"Is this what you want Cory are you sure this is the profession you want I just worry about you on the down side I have some friends who have gone a bit wacko in the head because they can't cope or handle the adult Industry I don't want you to go down that road". Oh don't you start I said my friend back home said the same about his friends who work in the industry that they have gone a little mad.

"I just worry about you Cory there is going to be lots more sex to come lots more scenes to do and lots more studios calling you up can you handle it? I guess all I can do is keep my eye on you I am here for you Cory day and night and night and day in fact you can move in with me it will be company for us both ok". Move in with you I said but, "stop worrying I don't want a fucking boyfriend I just want a warm loving friend who is not as crazy as I am! But is more crazy than I am (we both laughed). I moved in with Billy and we became very close.

Billy often had parties and lots of guys came to the parties who were in the porn Industry there were also a lot of drugs at the parties which I never took part in Billy always tried to get me to take some drugs but I would always profusely refuse it just was not my thing.

Billy used to point out all the different guys at the party he would say "see him sat over there on the couch well he is Bi - sexual he has a wife and two kids he does both the gay porn and straight porn and then he pointed to another guy see him having a drink he is not out about his sexuality but is a closet gay porn star." But I said wouldn't people who knew him know about his job. "Well no said Billy not unless they were looking for it and they were gay themselves". Then he pointed to two guys who were a couple and had met through the porn Industry it happens he said!

I said so many different people here leading different lives but they all have the same thing in common or we all have the same thing in common we all work in the adult entertainment Industry.

"It's a job said Billy to us it's a job it's work and it's our profession some other guys have other jobs too and they do porn work on the side just to make up the money why people think of it as disgust or a job only people out of their minds would go into I will never know. There are some really talented people in this Industry: writers, photographers, artists. Some talented minds here we are all human beings you know.

Billy tried to get me to snort some drugs but I said no Billy never will that shit go up my nose some guys at the party were snorting the drugs off some men's arse's as a kind of a kinky fetish but I guess it was that type of party.

I would always call my parents just to listen to their voices which made me feel better and made me feel loved I mean I was their son and I worked in the gay porn Industry and they accepted me for it what more support and love could I ask for these were god loving holy conservative parents who had a son like me and they love me just as much as they used too they never came to see me in Los Angeles though I think it was just too much for them to see me in Los Angeles and the life I now lived.

Dominic wanted to come to Los Angeles for a visit and a tour of the studio's I worked for it was a far cry from Salem Oregon, or even Alabama I told him of course he can and he knew a couple of guys in the Industry anyway I think Dominic was a little jealous of me going into the porn Industry and having my body all over the Internet he was worried about me at first because I think he thought I would not see it through but I did which I shocked myself. Dominic was stuck on the farm helping his dad like I could have wasting the years away and being sad because I was not gutsy enough to enter a profession I so much wanted to be part of he was longing to come to LA and see a different life all together.

Billy lived the high life and when he was not working he was calling everybody to a party and if he was not calling a party he was out getting fucked I just could not keep up with his hectic and full life.

I was getting plenty of work from loads of studios and I was doing all sorts of scenes for different studios I was a young boy being punished by my mature gym teacher for forgetting my gym shoes where I was tied up lying on my stomach having all sorts of pain inflicted on my ass which I will not go into in writing.

I was then for another studio the same day a naughty house boy and I was giving the owner of the house plenty of sex for extra cash his wife then came home and went berserk and he fucked her right in front of me and fucked me straight after (I thought who makes up these stories) Or are they even made up!.

I then got a call from another studio asking me if I would be Interested in pseudo-masochism (deep bondage), where I would be put through a lot of pain and torture by a lot of guys but the money was very good it was explained to me what the scenes would be (after all these are all controlled environments with a lot of specialist cameramen and professional porn stars or some amateur porn stars too) and it was very very kinky fetish stuff which I just could not go through with it was just too deep a fetish for me to do so I turned it down I was told they already have two other guys who are very very interested but they wanted me to be this part and I said no it was just way out of anything I would do in my profession. They were not happy at all and told me it was something I would regret but I stuck to my guns I was just in no way confident or comfortable enough to be put through all of that. The guys who would do this must be way, way out there.(It just goes to show how far some sex can actually go and what a lot of people out there are into but it was certainly not for me).

I came home from the studio to find Billy curled up into a ball in the corner of the room and crying the house was dark and I had never seen Billy like this before he was normally the life and soul of the house and did not stop talking but today he was a person I never thought I would see. "I said Billy what's going on what has happened" he looked up at me his eyes were red and swollen where he had been crying and I could see on the table powder (drugs) where he had been snorting. "Oh Cory he said I am finished I am fucking finished" "What do you mean, why" "I have just found out I am HIV positive" "But how you always use condoms for every shoot" "It was a one night stand a one night fucking stand a quick shag I have contacted the guy he never knew he was HIV himself oh fuck!.

"Look Billy they can treat HIV today with medication which keeps it dormant I mean you can even have sex with this medication it's amazing what they can do today". "Oh said Billy what am I going to do now, oh fuck".

"I said the first thing we do is go into therapy I will come with you for every session and we will get past this you need to learn how to live with this and I will help you, you are strong Billy you are very strong and I have always looked up to you for it please don't let me down because you're HIV positive."

Billy clutched me and held onto me for dear life he said "please don't leave me I need you I have never needed anybody but I need you more than ever now". "Billy I am here for you all the way ok and a bit of therapy might help me too (we both laughed).

"I said have you contacted work about your condition", "yes and I have decided to pull out of the Industry or do something in the Industry which does not Involve sex" "I said like what" "well they are always looking for story writers for scenes and I am thinking about that working behind the camera" (Billy was so confident and happy being on camera and he was a perfectionist with his scenes he was well respected by many studios and the profession loved him it was such a shame but he would make a brilliant story writer for the porn models to act out porn scenes).

For weeks and months Billy just hung around the house he was a different person completely to the Billy I knew when friends called he would not speak to them and he became a lonely recluse he clung to me in the nights and would lay on me in the evenings watching TV.

We went to every therapy session and I made sure Billy did not miss his medication his blood tests or his doctor appointments and we would go out in the evenings for a walk on the beach or a nice meal we were like a young couple but I knew Billy would get his confidence back in time and become the Billy he used to be it's amazing what something like this can do to a person's confidence and self - esteem but Billy would get it back in time because he was crazy Billy.

I worked in the day and came home at night and cooked for me and Billy and Billy spent his days writing scenes for porn studios he did not work in front of the camera but he used his wild and stinking imagination behind the camera.

Dominic called me and said "I am coming down to LA next week and asked if it is ok to stay with me and Billy" I asked Billy and he didn't really like it very much because for months it had just been me and him and that is how he wanted it I mean it worked for me too I hated the wild house party's he used to have and the company he used to keep now it was just a quiet and peaceful house to live in and as I say it worked for me. I was working doing my scenes so when I got home I needed the quiet time and Billy was now a writer so he needed the quiet too (great).

Billy said it was fine to ask Dominic to the house he said "fine it will be good to have a new face and personality about the place" (great I said).

Me and Billy never had sex with each other out of work and off camera. We just never got intimate with each other on a personal level. We were just the best of friends and that is how we kept it.

Dominic came to LA and Billy was right it was great to have a new face around the house I asked Dominic "so how is Oregon" "oh you know Oregon he said "Dominic wanted a tour of Los Angeles and he could not wait to see the wild nightlife that Los Angeles had to offer. I had to inform him of what had gone on with Billy and I asked him to just be quiet around the house as Billy was still very not himself at all and very much scared of how much he had changed but I guess life can do that to the best of us.

Dominic was looking forward to the wild parties I had told him about and the wild orgies that went on, on a regular basis at the house but of course all that had now changed.

I took Dominic to some of the gay porn studios and he was able to watch me work and when I would look at him I could see him laughing and holding his hands to his face I think it was just all great insight for him. Some of the guys in the studio asked Dominic if he would be interested in coming in to the business because he had a great body on him and model like looks and they loved his deep southern accent which was very very Southern Alabama but it was just not for him I think he loved all the sex part of it but not all the coverage over the Internet and on DVD's he told me "It would be too embarrassing to look back on in about 20 years time".

"yes but I said you can look back on it in about 20 years time and look at the great body you had and the sexual performances you used to give it will kind of live forever that is the power of technology."

"That's the positive he said, "That is the positive I said".

We decided to walk home from the studio that night because it was a lovely Los Angeles night and we stopped off for food in some restaurant when we got home all the lights in the house were off and Billy was nowhere to be seen. Me and Dominic looked all over for him we knew he would not have gone out because he was now very much a recluse and loner the next thing Dominic shouted at me "he's in bed" I walked into the bedroom and found Billy in a ball in the centre of his bed clutching onto the blankets and he was shaking and crying I could not understand it.

"I said Billy what is it what has happened" "he looked at me white as a ghost and said" one of my friends has killed himself he fucking cut his wrists this morning "Oh Billy I said I am so sorry apparently life just got too much for him his boyfriend of 10 years had left him and unbelievably gone back to his ex wife because they wanted to start again he called those 10 years" a phase he was going through "to finding out what he really wanted and he ruined a life in the process.

I sat with Billy all night just me and him on his bed talking and he kept on about how he just did not want to live anymore how he had given up on life and how he was thinking of ending it all. I grabbed his face and told him to look into my eyes and not take his eyes off mine I said to him "you will never do that to me ok you will never leave me (he burst out crying) I made him promise me that he must never leave me and I made him write it down on a piece of paper that he must keep his promise".

It was strange Billy was the strong one and he was the one that was supposed to be looking out for me but it kind of worked in the opposite direction I became the strong one for him and it kind of helped me too because I had to be strong for Billy and I had to stay positive so that gave me so much strength and confidence in myself.

Dominic did not want to go back to his ' mild ' life in Oregon so he asked myself and Billy if it was ok for him to stay with us In Los Angeles Billy did not mind and neither did I and we all got on really well together. In fact Billy got Dominic a Job in one of the studios as a receptionist and part time cleaner and Dominic got to see all the hunky male models coming and going throughout the day which he loved and very often dated. (Dominic was not shy with his chatting up lines and it was the right environment after all).

We all just got by day to day as best we could and we would take turns to cook and clean and we would eat together and go shopping together and talk most nights together and we would bring dates back to the house and they would Join us in our chats unfortunately Billy lost his confidence with dating but me and Dominic would very often find dates for him and we would drive him to the restaurant or wherever we would plan for them to meet.

Towards the end of many many dates between us we all found long term partners and I guess we are all happy in our own way. I think we all kind of found ourselves or maybe we still are trying to find ourselves in this hard world of ours only we are all a lot more comfortable now with ourselves and the future seems ok for us.

The only thing is between us we have a lot of underwear and socks which we all steal because we just don't know whose is who.

I don't know how much longer I am going to be in the gay porn Industry there is not much work now and new models are looking for work all the time and there is a lot of competition as there is with any business. There are certain things I will not do and I say no too, as I have my standards but there are a lot of models out there who will do the scenes and they get the parts.

I would not recommend going into the gay porn Industry but that is just me and that is my opinion we are all different and as I say that is my opinion and my opinion alone. What I can give you from this and my time in the Industry is just to be comfortable and confident in your own skin don't go into the Industry to find a way of escape from the "real world" because it is not an escape and if you're going into it to find something different then well it is different yes but you have to be in a good place and comfortable with your body and mind because the after effects on your mind and body if you are not in a good place going into the industry can have disturbing consequences and remember you are having sex on camera for the world to see and with a lot of people.

I guess a lot of gay porn models will disagree with me and say they loved and love their time in the Industry they got to meet and make friends for life it gave them a big break and it gave them fame and money these are all the positives and they are happy with doing this Job and they are happy with themselves which makes their futures in the Industry very ambitious and they are always looking for new sexual scenes and different people to do these scenes with.

You have to weigh up the pros and cons of everything in life.

But what advice could I give to the new up and coming generations of sexually active and curious young men who want to have a go or enter the world of gay porn all I would say to you is go into it being comfortable with your sexuality for a start, I would say love your body be in control with your mind and know what you want. I went into it because I wanted to I wanted to see what is what like and what is was all about I just had a passion for it and that passion just drove me to the Interview and then to the Industry. Many will go into it just for the fun of it to see what it is like and of course for the money but I was serious about it and you should be serious about it and it should be something you really want to do for only then will it become fun and you will love what you do.

Like anything in life there are mixed and different reviews but I guess we all have to find out individually because we are all different and unique.

On the whole if I ever do go to college or go into another profession my time in the gay porn Industry would have been a great experience for me because it was something I had to try and be part of whether it be long term or short term it was certainly an experience I will never forget and I was part of something that very few are I think lots of guys want to be part of it but many are also very afraid of it because of Judgment.

You can take from my story whatever you want to!

The End

www.ingramcontent.com/pod-product-compliance
Ingram Content Group UK Ltd.
Pitfield, Milton Keynes, MK11 3LW, UK
UKHW040020200726
13854UKWH00001B/278

9 781496 987860